A BURST OF GRAY

Cover image used courtesy of
Engin Akyurt

ISBN: 9781020001253 (Paperback)
ISBN: 9781020001291 (Ebook)

First Edition

Library of Congress Control Number: 2021917099

10 9 8 7 6 5 4 3 2

45 Alternate Press, LLC
www.45alternate.com

A BURST OF GRAY

A NOVEL IN 100-WORD STORIES

RAN WALKER

CONTENTS

For Elle and Zoë
And
In Memory of Dr. Bruce Cole

PREFACE

Several years ago I decided to try the idea for this book as a project for National Novel Writing Month (NaNoWriMo). To make it even more interesting, I decided to write it longhand. I wrote for a week, often times taking meandering turns that I feared I would be unable to properly fix, so I abandoned it.

My brother, Torrey, who is a voracious reader of sci-fi and fantasy, took a liking to the universe, though. In the end, that was the affirmation I needed. I figured whatever issues I was having with the book had more to do with me than the core idea of the book.

In the years since, I moved from writing long fiction to writing microfiction. In fact, since the fall of 2018, I have only written microfiction, most of my work between 50 and 100 words. It was only while I was doing the final edits on my 100-word story collection, *Keep It 100*, that the idea crossed my mind to try the idea for *A Burst of Gray* as a novel written in one hundred 100-word stories.

Rather than wrestle with how difficult it would be to execute such an idea, I just imagined the first scene of the book and wrote it as a 100-word story. That first one gave me confidence, and I quickly added on more stories until I got to a point where I was eager to know how this story would play out for the rest of the narrative arc.

The end result is what you're holding in your hands right now. An experiment in fiction. A new way of reading a novel that stems from a new way of writing one.

By definition, a novel should have 50,000 words or more, and by definition, a chapter shouldn't consist of exactly 100 words. But when you're doing something new, you have to sometimes rearrange your thinking. I have allowed myself to look at a book of exactly 10,000 words and see in it the complexity of something far longer.

I hope that you will do the same.

"The color of truth is gray."

ANDRÉ GIDE

ONE

MOM REMOVES her Chromatic glasses with a heavy sigh and places them on the dinner table between us. I know she misses Dad. I do, too.

Still, it irks me when she inadvertently shows me her privilege.

"The colors are faded, and these damn glasses don't do a thing!"

I gently take her hand in mine.

This response causes her to shake her head and apologize. "I'm sorry. Sometimes I forget."

Mom is not like the rest of us. She's different in that she's one of a small group of people in the world who can truthfully see in *color*.

TWO

My PARENTS MET and fell in love, and because they were actually soulmates, they became Chromats.

I'm happy they were able to experience this world in glorious colors I can't even imagine. I guess that's why I hold out hope it'll happen for me.

I carry a Color Card in the event I'm ever within 100 feet of my soulmate. That way I can know what colors I am seeing.

This is a long shot, I know. Mom agrees and encourages me to just settle down and start a family.

She wants to have grandchildren. I, however, want true love.

THREE

CHROMATIC GLASSES WERE CREATED to combat chromatic degeneration, which is usually the result of a soulmate dying, but can also be a byproduct of age. The glasses aren't meant to be a substitute for full color vision, but to lessen the impact of the change. The fact Chromats can still see colors makes this a "first world" problem, though.

I see thousands of tones and don't feel I'm missing anything. But my mother tells me otherwise.

So I'm still trying to win the Chromatic lottery at 40.

Maybe I've missed my window to find a companion by playing these odds.

FOUR

OUTSIDE OF MOM, I don't know any other Chromats.

When I was growing up, my parents were the only Chromats any of my friends knew personally. We'd sit around asking them questions about the colors of items in the house.

My best friend, Indigo, married his high school sweetheart twenty years ago. They now have three lovely children. Color has never been a part of any of their lives.

I have trouble with the idea of marrying someone who is not my soulmate, though. That's why I am alone.

I'm not blaming my parents.

I just want what they had.

FIVE

CURRENT SCIENCE SUGGESTS that if you're within 100 feet (30.48 meters) of your *dedicated chromadyadic symbiont* ("soulmate"), your vision will shift in both tone and hue. If you two can consummate a physical and emotional bond during the chromatic inception window (usually 30 days), the change will be permanent; otherwise, it will be temporary and lost after the inception window.

This is all way over my head, but I believe in the science. I believe in true love. I believe in a life with color.

Why are we built this way if we're not meant to desperately seek out love?

SIX

GIVEN the minuscule portion of the population that are Chromats, it's astonishing how much power and influence they wield for simply seeing things "as God intended." Many are elected to positions of power, and even a high school dropout can easily land a seven-figure salary as a Chromat.

Chromats call people like me Color Chasers. We are consumed by the act of encountering new people. Our lives are organized around it. Some of us even attend worldwide conventions, like Color-Fest, that systematically move crowds through large spaces in order to maximize the chances of chromatic inception.

Anything for love, right?

SEVEN

THE CRUELEST TRICK the universe has played is not allowing the children of Chromats to inherit the Chromatic gene. When it comes to finding a soulmate, you're on your own.

There are people who will never be in the same country as their soulmate. There are people whose soulmates will die before they're found. There are so many probabilities as to why the idea of a Chromat could be seen as a conspiracy theory, a big grift pulled off by the people in power.

Then there're my parents, two people who painted the sky with the truest colors of love.

EIGHT

THERE WAS ONCE A GIRL. I'd be tempted to say she was "the one," but science told me otherwise.

I cared for her deeply, as she did me, and we wanted to be together, sharing the world we already knew.

But I just couldn't.

What if one day while we were walking with our kids in the mall and suddenly I was struck with color?

I couldn't do that to her—or to myself.

A part of me wanted to hold on to what we shared, but I guess, in the end, I'm just too much of a Color Chaser.

NINE

INDIGO INVITES me to accompany him and his wife to a soiree downtown. I agree, because it will get me out of my one-bedroom apartment for a few hours.

It's a formal event, so I take out my darkest tux and brightest shirt. I decide to be daring with my bowtie, so I put on one that Mom tells me is the color *red*. She says that it's a strong, powerful color.

I check my wallet for my Color Card, in the off chance I run into my soulmate, although, honestly, I'd have a better chance of winning the lottery.

.

TEN

Most of the people I know are, ironically, named after colors. Even my name, Slate, is a color. I think my parents gave me that name so I wouldn't stick out from the other kids and highlight the fact that *they're* Chromats.

For most of us, our names might very well be the closest we ever get to seeing *colors*, which I will admit are mostly theoretical concepts.

I know one thing is certain: if I ever find my soulmate and become a Chromat, I'm going to find as many slate-colored things as I can and surround myself with them.

ELEVEN

Sometimes I have dreams where I imagine I am seeing things in color. As the settings blend into each other, I imagine that I am meeting her and her beauty is exploding into a million hues. I shield my eyes, feeling like a naked child entering the world, trembling at the air touching every pore of my skin, all at the same time.

I am new.

The world is the same, but somehow I am now more alive within it.

I hold her in my arms, and she places a kiss upon my lips.

I wake up, lips still tingling.

TWELVE

INDIGO AND ROSE seem so happy that I am left dumbfounded they are not Chromats. Their love appears, to me, as pure as the love my parents shared.

It's at moments like this that I question if I am not wasting my life chasing something completely unattainable. At my age, surely settling down would be the easiest option.

I watch Indigo and Rose, fingers interlocked, as we make our way through the ballroom to our table. I am a third wheel to their beautiful evening, the object of their pity.

I want to leave, but I know that I won't.

THIRTEEN

MOM LIKES to tell the story of how she and Dad met. She was at a concert—a legendary funk band that was touring with a full stage show, inclusive of space ships and guitarists dressed only in diapers— and during one of the band's many anthems, colors flooded her eyes. At first she thought it was some stage effect. Somehow in that crowd, Dad was drawn to her, and as the two of them two-stepped in an ocean of afro-ed people, they planted the seeds that would eventually lead to my being here.

That's quite a story, I know.

FOURTEEN

LIKE MY PARENTS, I'm a middle school teacher (Language Arts), unlike most people in this room. Even Indigo and Rose are entrepreneurs, selling insurance from an office out of their home.

I try to ignore the feeling of not belonging by scanning the crowd for single women, but this doesn't appear to be the kind of place where people connect like that.

I politely excuse myself from the table. I figure I can walk around in the lobby until the program begins, clear my head, stretch my legs.

As I approach the ballroom exit, my eyes flash —and I fall.

FIFTEEN

"You all right?" Indigo asks, helping me to my feet. "You took quite a spill."

I blink hard. "My card! My card!"

"What are you talking about?"

I reach in my pocket and retrieve the Color Card and stare at it like I've never seen it before.

"You carry one of those things around with you?" Indigo says. "Wait. You can see *colors*?"

I nod furiously.

"Damn. She's really here!"

I look around, my eyes racing with colors I've never seen before.

"Slate, look for a woman who just got here. She's probably just as disoriented as you," Indigo says.

SIXTEEN

No one is more disoriented than I.

I rush toward the ballroom door, nearly crashing through it. Thankfully, I don't run over anyone.

There are a few people milling about in the hallway, but there is one breath-taking woman who is curiously positioned just inside the lobby. It's as if someone yelled "freeze" and she just halted immediately, refusing to move a single muscle.

In my gut, I know it's her.

"Hey!" I yell, waving my arms and walking toward her.

She looks directly into my eyes, but rather than smile, she sprints right past me into the crowded ballroom.

SEVENTEEN

I HAVEN'T ALLOWED myself to believe my soulmate wouldn't be as excited as I am, but she looks terrified.

I slowly walk back into the ballroom, attempting to mask my disappointment.

There're so many questions I want to ask her, but those questions are quickly merging with the desire to stare at my Color Card and make sense of everything I'm seeing.

Soon the program starts, so I ease back to my table, eager to find her. It doesn't take long. Across the room, she steps onto the dais, greeting different people, before taking a seat in a reserved chair.

EIGHTEEN

I INSTINCTIVELY KNOW she is wearing red. The color is so striking and powerful—just like Mom described it. I tug at my bowtie and realize that I am right.

Her skin glows, as the chandelier lights dance upon its smoothness. Her long, dark hair is curly, and her beauty is ethereal. The saying 'love at first sight' was birthed from a moment like this, I'm now absolutely certain of it.

She is seated next to an older man who is wearing shades. She reaches for his hand and he takes hers. He then caresses it gently, before kissing it.

NINETEEN

"ARE YOU ALL RIGHT?" Indigo asks. Rose pats my shoulder, so I know she's aware I am now Chromatic. Even in my confusion, I can see just how beautiful a couple they really are.

I nod, but I know they can see through this.

I stare at the dais, wondering who she is and how after forty years I am just now running into her. Then I turn my attention toward the man holding her hand.

It is then that I see the wedding rings.

My heart feels like it is falling off a cliff with no ground in sight.

TWENTY

I REFUSE to take my eyes off her, but I notice that she won't even look at me. I can sense her trepidation, even from this distance.

Her eyes remain fixed on her husband, who appears oblivious to her gaze.

I vaguely hear the emcee introduce the speaker for the evening, Donovan Scott, as the older man begins to rise. She rises with him, one arm around his waist, the other on his arm, and escorts him to the podium. It is only then that I realize he is blind.

She returns to her seat, and he begins to speak.

TWENTY-ONE

DONOVAN SCOTT TALKS about "the unconquerable human spirt," sharing brief anecdotes from his life and how he overcame blindness to not only find his soulmate, but to also build a thriving construction empire. The speech walks a fine line between bragging and encouragement, exuding the confidence of a powerful man.

But he said *soulmate*.

If she is my soulmate, it is scientifically impossible for her to be his. Everyone knows this.

That's when I realize that his being blind would mean he would have to rely solely on what she has told him.

He believes she is already a Chromat.

TWENTY-TWO

MY EYES NEVER LEAVE HER, and eventually hers meet mine.

She is finally seeing me. We are finally taking each other in.

I want to know her story, why she chose to marry Donovan Scott, what their marriage is like, whether they have children.

Why did she choose to build a life on a lie?

Money? Power?

Who is this woman the universe has intended me to share my life with, this woman who gave up on me long before today?

Can I even bring myself to commit my life to a woman who has chosen to live this way?

TWENTY-THREE

BUT JUDGMENT IS something I don't have the benefit of dwelling on. I have waited forty years for this moment.

Our gazes continue, and with each passing moment, my mixed feelings begin to dissolve.

I am entranced.

While there is a part of me that is excited about the possibility of learning the names of these colors using my Color Card, I don't want to look away. I realize I am building a memory of this moment, my eyes overflowing with colors and beauty.

Maybe it won't hurt to say hello, though a part of me knows that's not enough.

TWENTY-FOUR

I count the seconds until the program ends and she and her husband rise from the dais.

I rush to meet them before they reach the door, but it feels as though this color-blinding throng of people is working systematically to keep me from getting near them.

Indigo whispers to Rose, then nods to me. "Follow me," he says, bulldozing his way through suits and evening gowns, apologizing along the way. I follow him like a running back trailing an offensive lineman.

We reach the Scotts as they enter the lobby.

I have no idea of what I will say.

TWENTY-FIVE

"Mr. Scott," I say, placing a hand gently on his shoulder, "I really enjoyed your speech." I glance at my soulmate nervously. "Very inspiring."

"Well, thank you. Glad my words were well received."

"Indeed, sir."

Suddenly she drops her purse on the floor in front of me.

"Sorry," she says to him, while looking at me.

"No problem. I'll get it," I offer, kneeling down to retrieve her purse.

I hand it to her and she touches my hand gently, imperceptibly, and places something into my palm.

"Thank you," she says.

"Yes, thank you," he repeats, as they walk away.

TWENTY-SIX

Indigo heads back for Rose, leaving me standing in the lobby alone, staring at the tiny piece of paper in my hand. On this sheet are her name and what appears to be her phone number. Her name is Jade.

I already know that I will call her, though there is a part of me that feels it would be wrong for me to do that. Still, she gave me her number, and I need to know why.

As I ponder this, the colors before my eyes begin to fade back to normal, signaling she has already left the building.

TWENTY-SEVEN

WHEN I GET HOME, it takes everything in me not to call her. I can't risk it. Instead, I lie on my bed, attempting to remember as much as I can from that evening, including the moment I first saw Jade.

I try to imagine a world in which I had found her in time to be with her. I imagine what it would feel like to kiss her, to make love to her. I imagine us navigating this world as a couple, two people the universe intended to be together.

I wonder if she is thinking about me, too.

TWENTY-EIGHT

ONE OF THE benefits of being a teacher is that you have the summers off. This is both a blessing and a curse. You have time to decompress, but often times it feels like too much time to be without a real purpose.

The absence of my classes leaves me with an inordinate amount of time to fixate on my experience last night. Jade's number sits on the kitchen counter, daring me to call. Instead, I live a million lifetimes in the curves of her cursive, the strokes of her pen, movements that I never noticed her making last night.

TWENTY-NINE

I CONSIDER TELLING Mom about my Chromatic experience, but I don't want to break her heart with the reality of it all. I am comforted only by the fact that I have 29 days left to be around Jade before being a Chromat is no longer an option.

It is then that I see why she gave me her number.

We can use this bit of science to enjoy the Chromatic experience, knowing we would be unable to keep it without completely committing ourselves to each other.

My guilt is assuaged by this idea.

This is no longer about love.

THIRTY

THE PHONE RINGS so long I fear I will need to leave a voicemail. Then her voice abruptly breaks the ringing.

"Yes."

"It's me. Slate. From last night."

Her voice is distant, as if she is talking to someone other than me. "I have to run some errands today. I'll pick up the frame from Cyan's around four, but then I have some other errands to run."

The phone suddenly clicks and the line goes dead.

Was she talking to me or him?

Slowly it dawns on me that she was speaking to both of us.

It's almost three.

THIRTY-ONE

CYAN'S IS an art supply store, roughly forty miles away in a city I rarely visit. I only know it's there because I've had to purchase things for my classes in the past.

I pull into the parking lot at 3:45 and wait. I listen to music, doing my best to sooth my growing anxiety. I'm hoping I didn't misunderstand her words.

Like a light switch getting flipped on, the colors come flooding back before my eyes.

I turn off my car and approach the door, trying not to rush my movements. I see her in the distance, looking away.

THIRTY-TWO

I FOLLOW her to the back of the store, where I see her examining frames.

I approach her slowly, carefully.

"Hi. I'm Slate," I say extending my hand to her.

She takes it, then quickly releases it. "Slate, what do you think of this frame?"

I turn my eyes toward the frame, confused. "It's nice, I guess."

"Slate, I'm Jade. It's best that we not talk. Let's just enjoy being around each other."

It's difficult to mask my disappointment.

"I have to purchase this frame. Then I'm going to the bookstore down the street."

She wants me to follow her.

THIRTY-THREE

I LINGER around Cyan's while she makes her purchase, then head back to my car. I follow her luxury sedan in my small hatchback, fighting my disappointment through the amazement of colors surrounding me. I even see random, jarring color collages on the sides of buildings.

If Jade doesn't want to actually get to know me, then I can take that time to familiarize myself with my Color Card.

I know all of this is futile, if I'll lose my ability to see color anyway, but in the days I have Chromatic vision, I want to understand what I'm seeing.

THIRTY-FOUR

WE PARK three cars away from each other in the parking lot of Goreman Books. I follow her without appearing to follow her.

She sets up her things at a small table in the back of the cafe. I grab a few magazines and sit two tables away. She quietly pulls out her own Color Card and puts on a pair of reading glasses, as she peruses the art books on her table. I decide to do the same.

Occasionally I glance up at her. I've never seen a woman as beautiful as she.

I sigh and lower my head.

THIRTY-FIVE

AFTER HALF AN HOUR, she rises from the table and glances at me.

Obediently, I follow her to the back of the bookstore in a small nook that is hidden from plain view.

"I know this is not what you expected," she says to me, finally looking into my eyes. "But I am married to a very powerful man, and he's incredibly jealous. I can't risk it."

I nod.

"Call me in two days. At noon. I'll answer. Listen for a place and time. Okay?"

I nod.

"Slate, I'm really sorry."

I nod.

We walk back to our respective cars.

THIRTY-SIX

I UNDERSTAND THE SITUATION, but I still struggle to see the upside for what we are doing.

What if I did try to get to know her? After all, we *are* soulmates.

It's not her fault that she saw fit to marry Donovan Scott and move on with a life she felt would be good for her. Still, as I replay the handful of words she spoke to me today, I sense that she is not entirely happy at home.

It's a loose thread I so desperately want to pull.

But if I do, everything may very well fall apart.

THIRTY-SEVEN

Indigo is unable to mask his pity for me. He has followed my quest for many years now, at one point even contemplating whether to commit to Rose. He, being far more pragmatic than I, decided to build a life with someone who was not his soulmate.

"You guys looked amazing at the banquet," I say. "You're the color of copper, and Rose is the color of sepia. Your skin tones are beautiful together."

"Ha!" Indigo says, smiling.

Even though it doesn't really matter, I can tell he's happy to know that they managed this in spite of the universe.

THIRTY-EIGHT

OVER OUR WEEKLY LUNCH, I am reticent about sharing the fact that I've been shadowing my soulmate because she is already married. This is not the story I'd hoped for. This is not the story Mom wanted for me.

Mom twirls her Chromatic glasses in her hand, as if she's considering throwing them against the wall across the restaurant.

"Did Dad have to win you over, even though you knew he was your soulmate?" I ask.

"There's only so much the universe can do. The rest is up to us."

I take her words home with me, wrestling with them.

THIRTY-NINE

THIS NORMAL WORLD is all I've ever known, so I don't know why I'm suddenly fearing that this will become my permanent existence. I guess my problem is that I've never accepted my *normal*.

I don't want to let go of what I've spent my life searching for, and there's a part of me that knows, deep down, Jade doesn't want to either.

Why else would she torture herself with an ability she can only have around me for three more weeks?

But even I know Chromatic vision isn't enough to keep two people together, unless they choose to be.

FORTY

I CALL JADE, and she mentions a botanical garden over an hour away.

Of course I will be there.

I have always heard that one of the true benefits of being Chromatic is taking in an array of flowers and plants, seeing them in their natural splendor. Frankly, I'm surprised it took us a week to come here.

As I sit in the parking lot, her sedan pulls up next to me. She's gotten a lot more comfortable with this, I can tell.

For a moment we stare at the brilliant colors bursting before us. Then we exit our cars.

FORTY-ONE

BECAUSE THERE ARE no shelves or tables, we must actually walk, jointly, through the maze of azaleas, roses, and wildflowers.

"I believe this color is pink," she says, pointing at an azalea.

I smile, surprised. "I just learned that my skin is the color of chestnut. Who would've thought?"

She laughs. "I'm cinnamon."

"Suddenly I'm hungry."

She laughs again, this time touching my arm.

"What color most surprises you?" I ask.

"Cobalt blue. It feels electric."

"If you see it today, can you point it out?"

"Sure," she responds.

We continue our conversation, moving about the expanse of the garden.

FORTY-TWO

WE CIRCLE the entire garden three times before she admits she has to get home.

"I'm actually surprised he hasn't called to check on me yet."

Since we have been together for nearly two hours nonstop, I have noticed how compatible we really are—which shouldn't have been a surprise.

"Can I ask you a question?"

"Sure."

"Why did you marry him?"

She looks at me with a mixture of animosity and curiosity, but does not respond.

We continue walking.

"I wish I could take Chromatic vision home with me so I could relive today."

She sighs. "So do I."

FORTY-THREE

WHEN I GET BACK to my apartment, I turn off the lights and lie down on my bed, the ceiling fan sweeping the June air over me. I imagine Jade lying down beside me, telling me more about herself: her favorite things, the passions that burn within her.

Like me, she has no children, though neither of us would reveal why we chose not to have them. Our lives, even in this current funky predicament, still, oddly, complement each other.

I imagine her kiss would be unlike any kiss I've ever experienced.

Why do I keep doing this to myself?

FORTY-FOUR

THE PHONE RESTS inches from my hand, and I want so desperately to communicate with her. I wonder what she is doing right now, how she is being treated, whether she wishes she were here, lying on my bed, staring at this dark ceiling, like a night sky that extends through space and time.

I close my eyes and imagine our fingers inter-locked, our bodies rising through the sky, through a kaleidoscope of colors that we have yet to learn the names of.

When I am with her, I feel safer than I ever have.

I hope she does, too.

FORTY-FIVE

W̲E̲ ̲R̲E̲T̲U̲R̲N̲ to the botanical garden and find a hidden gazebo where we can talk.

She immediately apologizes for how she reacted to my last question. I offer my own apology for prying too much.

"I was thirty and beginning to fear I'd be alone. Then Donovan came along. He was successful, but I knew he wouldn't want anything to do with a girl from the South Side."

"So you convinced him he was your soulmate?"

She lowers her head, ashamed. "I know it wasn't right, but I was tired of being alone. I didn't think I'd ever find you."

FORTY-SIX

WE SIT SIDE BY SIDE, beneath an arch of flora, our hands touching.

"Do you love him?" I ask.

She looks down and away. "What does love matter at this point?"

"Is there a chance that *we* could be more than *this*?"

"I've made my choices. Now I have to live with them." She lifts her gaze to the horizon ahead of us.

"I can't stop thinking about you," I say.

She sits quietly for a moment before responding, "Me, too."

This time she faces me, and something almost chemical pulls us together.

Our lips touch and the world evaporates.

FORTY-SEVEN

THAT NIGHT I fall asleep with her kiss still tingling upon my lips. I had never tasted perfection until that moment. All of the frustration, the guilt, the anger, the feelings of failure, they all dissolved like sugar crystals into a brewing tea.

I feel brand new, as if I have never experienced another woman in my life, as if I would never want to experience another woman in my life.

I have never been in love before, where my heart felt such a dependency on another person, but now I have trouble imagining any kind of life without her.

FORTY-EIGHT

INDIGO LISTENS TO MY STORY, his befuddled expression deepening with each passing word. I know he wants to celebrate these small victories with me, but he also is keenly aware of the flip side to all of this: I am a heartbeat away from having a full-blown affair.

"Do you really love her—so soon?" he asks.

"Yes."

"Do you think she loves you, too?"

"I don't know."

Indigo takes a deep breath. "This is unchartered territory for me. Rose and I dated for three years before we got married."

I start to say the obvious, but he already knows.

FORTY-NINE

DURING OUR STANDING LUNCH DATE, Mom remarks how something about me is different, more confident. I know I don't have to explain any of this. She'll let it pass, if I want her to, but I decide to let her know the deal. I'm in too deep to not come clean with her.

I expect her judgment, my stomach already clinched at the idea I've elected to disappoint her. Her response surprises me, though.

"It's really something, isn't it?" she muses.

Over lunch Mom tells me about her experiences loving Dad, happy to finally share her story with another Chromat.

FIFTY

Maybe it's Mom's response still ringing in my ears, but sitting with Jade in what has become our special place, I confess that I want to be with her, that I want to find a way to make this work out.

In many ways this is unfair of me. Still, I want her to know she has a choice. We are now down to our final two weeks.

"There's not enough time. There's so much left for us to do," she responds.

"But we don't have to let this end."

Her tear-filled eyes mirror my own, our kisses like saltwater.

FIFTY-ONE

I DRIVE HOME in a rush of euphoria, trying to figure out how this could work. Do we leave and go off the grid so that no one finds us?

That doesn't make sense.

We both have responsibilities. Plus, what kind of life is it when you have to constantly look over your shoulder?

Up till this point, I have thought very little about what any of this would do to Donovan Scott, but I am reminded when I check my phone and realize I have a message from an unknown caller.

I sense who it is before I listen.

FIFTY-TWO

"I DON'T NOW who you are, but you'd better stop calling my wife's phone. Don't let me find out who you are."

Although my stomach is in knots, I play the message again.

Under any other situation, I would tuck my tail and count my losses, but Jade and I are soulmates. This is different. I can't just walk away.

I have to remind myself that he believes she is *his* soulmate and that I am tampering with their Chromatic bond, even though he is unable to use it.

This is a bad time to have not developed a plan.

FIFTY-THREE

INDIGO AND ROSE invite me over to have dinner with their family. I haven't seen my godson, Ash, in a month, so I eagerly accept.

After we have dinner and Ash and I play with his latest toy race cars, Indigo, Rose, and I settle down for a drink in the living room.

"I can't believe you're doing this," Rose says to me.

"Baby, this is his only chance at love," Indigo responds.

She looks at him incredulously. "So what do *we* have?"

I hate to see them torn over my actions.

"Rose, what do you think I should do?"

FIFTY-FOUR

Outside of Mom, I never consulted a woman about what I'm doing. There's an entire perspective that has eluded me. Indigo is operating from a space of us having been friends since childhood. Rose is the more pragmatic one at this point.

"It's not fair to her husband," Rose says.

"But she doesn't love him. She loves me," I say.

"There's still right and wrong."

Indigo starts to say something to help me out, but he realizes he's already in the doghouse for his earlier comment.

"If the tables were turned, would you want another man to steal *your* wife?"

FIFTY-FIVE

As I DRIVE HOME, the sky seems heavier than before, the clouds drunk with melancholy, their bellies full and aching.

I replay all the things Rose told me. There's a part of me that wants to say that being soulmates trumps it all, as if this mere fact can somehow magically undo the feelings and emotions one person has developed for another. I have to remind myself that Jade and I are in an elite group of people to even have this concern.

When I reach my apartment, I am left with a single question: can I let Jade go?

FIFTY-SIX

THE UNIVERSE KNOWS it's not enough for chromodyadic symbionts to want to be together. They must consummate their monogamous union and dwell together, forsaking all others, at the risk of losing chromaticism.

I used to wonder if the universe watched over us like a strict parent to make sure we played by the rules humans are more than ready to ignore.

Actually, it's a wonder Chromats even exist, given how life bends into various shapes.

Oddly, civil or religious ceremonies matter very little in this situation. It's all about the chemistry of human beings, those feeble creatures preordained to fail.

FIFTY-SEVEN

FOR MORE THAN 14,610 DAYS, I have experienced a normal life, a life of tones and shadows.

I have seen beautiful things. I have had fun times. If not for the idea of being Chromatic, I would have lived a happy life, completely oblivious to what I was missing.

If I had different parents, things might've been different. But I can't blame them. There's just this restlessness inside of me.

I should count myself lucky I ever saw a world of color, treat it like a bucket list item, and accept the world that has always been there for me.

FIFTY-EIGHT

MY PHONE RINGS repeatedly from an unknown number, and I feel like a coward for not answering. I finally work up the courage to check my voicemail.

"Please meet me at our spot today at noon. I'll be there. I hope you get this message."

It's Jade's voice, although it's not her number. I glance at the time. It's already 10:45 AM.

I jump in my car, headed to the botanical garden. On the way, I call the number.

"Slate?" she answers.

"Yes?"

"I really need to see you now."

"I'm already headed that way."

"Be careful. I love you."

FIFTY-NINE

THOSE ARE the words that have lain beneath the surface for weeks now, but it is she, and not I, who has finally ventured to say them.

Knowing that Donovan Scott is already looking for me, I am sensing that Jade is in danger. There are a million questions I want to ask her, but her safety is paramount at this point.

I pull into the parking lot but don't see her car. Staring at the flora around me, I am stricken at how different the place looks.

I navigate my way to our spot, then sit down and wait.

SIXTY

NOON COMES AND GOES.

I stare at the flower petals. I am haunted by the fact that I now know their true colors, and I am reminded that this place was never designed for most of us.

I call Jade's number and it goes to a voicemail that hasn't been set up.

I look at the time again. She is nearly half an hour late.

Now I am worried.

I try to rein in my imagination, thoughts that frighten me to my core. Surely she is all right, I pray.

Then suddenly the flowers before me burst into bright pink.

SIXTY-ONE

PULCHRITUDE is a word that I never used to describe anything before. Somehow it feels superior to *beautiful*, reserved for something that would have been adored by even the gods.

Yet that is the only word that comes to mind as Jade approaches me, the red of her clothing a poem unto itself.

Her eyes are filled with a mixture of fear and desire. I rise to my feet and walk toward her.

Standing in the open, surrounded by the exploding colors of summer, we kiss each other in a way that I never knew possible, and the colors *intensify*.

SIXTY-TWO

I WANT to ask her a million questions, not the least of which is how she is holding up, but her kisses are intoxicating and I am unable to pull my lips away long enough to form the words.

When our lips finally part, the questions return like a flame tasting dry leaves.

"I was worried about you. The phone number. Your husband answering the phone."

She takes my hand and guides me toward the gazebo.

"I'm leaving him."

I feel guilty hearing this, although deep down I know for there to be an *us*, there can't be a *them*.

SIXTY-THREE

"HE KNOWS," I say shamefully.

"He suspects."

In this moment I now understand that she is the one with everything to lose, not me. I have always left space for this possibility, but she has not. Whatever happens now, I feel that I need to be an involved party.

"You want to run away with me?"

"Slate, this isn't a movie. We can't just disappear off the grid."

I nod. "I'll talk to him directly."

"I can't let you do that. He won't take that very well."

I appreciate her words, but we both know she can't do this alone.

SIXTY-FOUR

"Do you love him?" I finally bring myself to ask.

"He's good to me."

"How would this work?"

"Honestly, I never thought I'd meet my soul-mate. I don't know exactly how *this* works."

I explain to her about the pledge of monogamy and the consummation and how we have to live together. The words sound ludicrous when said aloud.

"And then we will remain Chromats?"

The question is innocuous, but suddenly it feels weighted, as if her motivations might extend beyond love.

"Yes."

She nods her head, absorbing my words.

Gently caressing my face, she says, "I have an idea."

SIXTY-FIVE

WE STARE out into the horizon, the sun an orangish hue, wrapped in a deep blue and a sliver of violet. I am transfixed on this natural beauty, trying to overcome my frustrations that only Chromats have been able to enjoy this to the point of disinterest.

Jade takes my hand in hers, and a gentle breeze finds its way to us, cooling us from the heat.

I want to ask if she ever did things like this with Donovan Scott, but I doubt it matters.

If she did, she never saw what the two of us are now seeing.

SIXTY-SIX

SHE ASKS me to trail her in my car. As we drive farther into the countryside, we converse over our mobile phones. She tells me she created an argument with Donovan Scott to give herself an excuse to go and stay with a cousin for a few days.

There are no relatives, though. She has told me the story of how she was alone and desperate to survive. But Donovan doesn't know this.

She pulls up to a small discreet motel, the kind of place one would flee to after robbing a bank.

We walk in and pay in cash.

SIXTY-SEVEN

BEING ALONE with her in this cramped room full of beiges and oranges is both exhilarating and scary. The door is locked, but it still feels like anyone could kick it in and catch us in flagrante delicto.

She senses my reticence and takes my hands in hers.

"This is what you wanted, what *we* wanted, right?"

I am unable to speak.

"Do you love me?" she asks, pulling me from my thoughts.

"Yes."

She smiles. "This is crazy! We've only known each other for a couple of weeks."

"Maybe that's the way this is supposed to work," I respond.

SIXTY-EIGHT

FACING EACH OTHER, we take each other's hands and pledge ourselves to each other. Unsaid is the fact that she managed to convince Donovan Scott she was his soulmate without doing any of this. The only reason I know these steps is because I have parents who are Chromats and I have studied this subject ad nauseam.

Our words are not scripted, but they come from the spaces in our hearts reserved for the other.

The next part has my stomach in knots. While it's not my first time being with a woman, this time feels both taboo and exhilarating.

SIXTY-NINE

SHE SLOWLY REMOVES her clothes and lies down on the bed. I want so desperately to make love to her, but there's a part of me that knows the likelihood of any of this working is slim, given that she's still married. How would the universe know? I don't know—but I sense it does.

"Let's just hold each other," I manage. "There'll always be time for this."

She nods, dejected, then dresses and lies down.

"I want us to be together," she says.

"I know," I respond, holding her closely, "but we have to do this the right way."

SEVENTY

We wake in the early hours of the morning to a heavy rapping on the door.

I glance through the keyhole and see three guys dressed in suits.

"Who is it?" Jade asks.

We are both dressed, having slept in our clothes.

"I think these men might be with your husband."

She grabs her purse and rushes toward the bathroom.

"What are you doing?"

"Trying to look like I didn't just spend the night with you."

"But we didn't do anything."

She doesn't respond because she already knows that it doesn't matter what has really happened.

We are alone together.

SEVENTY-ONE

ONCE SHE IS READY, I open the door. There is no way out, except through the front door. I am bracing myself to have to fight, but the man in the center says, "Mr. Donovan Scott would like to see you both. Come with us."

I look around for our cars in the parking lot and realize that Jade's sedan is gone. So is my hatchback.

"Hold on," I say, stepping back from the door.

I look at Jade. "What do we do?"

She reaches for my hand. "We go with them."

I grab the room key and we leave.

SEVENTY-TWO

WE ARE NOT BOUND or handcuffed, yet the restriction I feel is overwhelming. I look at Jade, who sits between me and one of the suited goons.

Neither of us says a thing. Instead we look down, our hands resting inches from each other. She told me before that her complexion is cinnamon, and I can't imagine a complexion more beautiful than this.

The silence of the SUV is interrupted by the driver clearing his throat as if he might speak, but he doesn't.

I have no idea of what to expect, but I am beginning to fear the worst.

SEVENTY-THREE

THE RIDE LASTS LONG ENOUGH for me to piece together how they found us. Her attempts to throw him off were never foolproof, but my guess is she didn't feel she would have to be so thorough. He followed the easiest breadcrumb he could: her sedan. There was no doubt a GPS on it, and rather than report the vehicle stolen, he opted to send his own people after us.

"Are you all right?" I whisper to Jade.

She nods but does not look directly at me.

This reaction instills greater fear in me than either of the three men.

SEVENTY-FOUR

WE PULL into the garage of a large building and are then ordered out of the car and escorted to an elevator that takes us directly to the penthouse floor.

Once we step off the elevator, I am astonished at how lavish and ornate the place is. In all this opulence rests a series of expensive-looking white porcelain figurines scattered about. Ironically, this is the kind of art that could be appreciated by anyone, not just Chromats.

Within minutes, Donovan Scott enters the room, walking casually, unassisted, clearly familiar with the room's layout.

"Please sit," he orders us.

We oblige.

SEVENTY-FIVE

"TELL me why I shouldn't have my men take care of you."

I had considered the possibility that this could end violently, but his words chill me to the bone.

"I would never do anything to hurt you. It's just that she is my soulmate."

"That's what I gathered," he responds.

He speaks out into the room. "Jade, do you take me for a fool?"

"No, Donovan. Not at all."

"You embarrass me like this? After all I have given you?"

She doesn't respond.

"You lied to me all these years. Did you ever love me?"

Her silence is deafening.

SEVENTY-SIX

"Was it your plan to run off together?"

I try to swallow, but I'm unable to. "I wanted to talk to you, man to man."

"And what exactly were you planning to say?"

"Sir, Jade is my soulmate."

"Yes. You mentioned that already."

"I don't know what else to say other than I am drawn to her, and in many ways, it's outside of my control."

"You know," he responds, "I wish you wouldn't hide behind that 'it's science' bullshit."

Snatching a porcelain figurine from the coffee table, he throws it into the wall, shattering it into a thousand pieces.

SEVENTY-SEVEN

"JADE, IS THIS WHAT YOU WANT?" he asks. He is not pleading. In fact, he is strangely detached.

She is staring at her clasped hands, tears streaming down her face. "Yes," she says softly.

"You two are really something."

He looks at one of his goons. "Get this guy's car ready for him downstairs."

He then looks in Jade's direction. "Take out your driver's license."

Her hands shaking, she complies.

"You're free to leave, but the only thing you're taking with you is that license. You can be with him, but you won't do it with anything I bought you."

SEVENTY-EIGHT

WE BOARD the elevator alone this time, and I take Jade in my arms. I can feel her shivering. As much as I want to promise her everything will be fine, I can't be sure. She'll come and live with me in my one-bedroom apartment across town, after having lived for years in a penthouse. She will be starting over, and I am the cause of that.

As we walk through the lobby, I see my beat-up hatchback in front of the building, an eyesore.

I open the passenger door for her, and she enters without looking at me.

SEVENTY-NINE

"I LOVE YOU," I say.

She hasn't spoken a word since she sat down. I am hoping my words will help to bring her out of her shell.

"I don't have any clothes," she finally says, wiping her eyes.

"I'll take you to get some right now."

She looks away from me, knowing that these clothes will be nothing like those in her penthouse closet.

I turn onto the highway, and a rainbow greets us in the distance. She stares at it, a slow smile beginning to spread across her face.

I reach for her hand, and she takes mine.

EIGHTY

WE DON'T WASTE any time getting back to my place. Before we do anything else, we know we have to finish pledging ourselves to each other. With only days left, we enter my bedroom and undress each other.

I take her in completely, pushing away every thought in my mind that is not connected to her. She looks back at me. I sense she is struggling to do the same.

I place my hands on her shoulders and gently caress her skin. She kisses me gently, wistfully.

We lie down and our bodies and minds merge into a single glow.

EIGHTY-ONE

IN SPITE OF OURSELVES, we find a satisfaction in this union.

Neither of us speaks, as our sweat-covered bodies lie across the strewn sheets, exhausted.

I know I should feel excited that we'll be Chromats going forward, but this moment is bittersweet. I had to tear apart a marriage for this to happen, the very definition of selfishness.

I keep these thoughts to myself, not wanting to poison the air with my guilty admissions.

Jade's head rests against my chest. I can feel her sweet exhalations sweeping across my chestnut skin, songs sung in a key only I can hear.

EIGHTY-TWO

"I was about ten when I realized there were two worlds: the haves and have nots," Jade says, as we sit facing each other on my bed. "I knew people like me didn't stand a chance at a life where I could experience color. It was unfair. They didn't have to tell us what we were missing, and we'd have been just fine."

Although I can relate, I sit quietly, listening. I want to learn as much about my soulmate as I can.

"Even though I was with him, there was always something missing—like I couldn't cheat the universe."

EIGHTY-THREE

"MY MOTHER WORKED two jobs to take care of me. When she got sick, it was my turn to step up. I worked all of these part-time jobs to keep the lights on and make sure the medical bills got paid. Then she died." Jade stops and looks away from me.

I rub her hand gently, my heart hurting for her.

"Even after Mom was gone, I was still in the same cycle of working random jobs. I tried to save for college, but that never happened. So I made the only play I could."

She, too, is haunted.

EIGHTY-FOUR

I TELL her about my mother and father, about my seemingly ridiculous pursuit of the impossible. She chuckles to herself as she weighs how we arrived at this exact moment in very different ways.

"I imagine every Chromatic couple has its own story, and ours is probably the least unusual," I say.

"Possibly." She smiles and I am lost in her doe-eyed gaze, completely vulnerable.

There are so many technical issues to work out with our living together, but I view these as "first-world" problems.

We have found each other. Against all odds, *we have found each other*.

EIGHTY-FIVE

THE NEXT TIME we make love, it feels less oblig-
atory, more natural. My flesh chases her flesh, our
bodies kissing, pressing, sliding, thrusting, seeking
the solace that has, up until that moment, eluded
us. I drink in her perfection, understanding I am
the one for whom each of these ideals and idiosyn-
crasies is designed to be appreciated. A tiny mole
on her shoulder. A dimple in one of her cheeks. A
birthmark on her thigh. All uniquely arranged
upon her body like words only I can read and sa-
vor. We give in to each other, building a sanctuary
of ecstasy.

EIGHTY-SIX

INEVITABLY WE MUST EMERGE from our cocoon to pick up clothes and other things she will need to be comfortable for the time being. We slide back into the clothes that lie crumpled on the floor beside the bed. As we walk to the car, I want to apologize again for not driving something more impressive—but I realize if I do, I will wind up eventually apologizing for everything in my life that doesn't reflect the life Donovan Scott gave her. That is a slippery slope I must avoid.

I open the door for her. She smiles in return.

EIGHTY-SEVEN

BENEATH A CLEAR BLUE SKY, sporadically punctu-
ated by fluffy white clouds, we cruise down the
highway. The river stretches out on either side of
the bridge ahead of us. We laugh into the wind
coming through our lowered windows, feeling alive
and free.

The cars up ahead are slowing to a halt.

When I press my brakes nothing happens. I
press the pedal to the floor. I quickly realize
someone must have done something to the brakes
while we slept.

Now we are flying out of control toward a
group of cars. At the last minute I swerve to avoid
them.

EIGHTY-EIGHT

My car crashes through the rail of the bridge like a roller coaster jumping the rails. Jade's screams fill my ears, and all I can think to do is reach for her hand as we fall for what feels like eternity before slamming into the water.

With the windows already down, water rushes into the car before I can hold my breath. I open my eyes through the darkness, unable to make out much in front of me.

I manage to unbuckle myself and reach for Jade, feeling for her belt clip. I push down and pull her toward me.

EIGHTY-NINE

I PULL Jade through the window after me, as the car continues to drop. She is not moving, and I feel myself starting to panic. I hold her beneath her arms and try to propel us toward the surface, my lungs burning for air.

I fear I won't make it to the surface before water fills my lungs.

After a few moments my head rises above the surface of the water. I gasp for air, lifting Jade's face to the sky. I hear sirens in the distance and vaguely notice people standing on the bridge looking down.

"Help!" I plead.

NINETY

I struggle to tread water with my free hand, while trying to inch Jade closer to a shore that seems invisible, given how far away it is. It's all futile. She needs CPR, but we're in the middle of the river.

"Help!" I scream repeatedly.

Finally someone from the bridge begins throwing emergency floatation devices into the water. I struggle to reach one of them, but once I have it, someone begins to pull us quickly.

From out of nowhere I see a boat racing toward us.

"She's not breathing!"

The next thing I know, we are being yanked upward.

NINETY-ONE

THE SUN IS BLINDING. I hear the EMTs giving Jade chest compressions, and time is drawing out slowly.

By the time they get her into the ambulance, she still has no pulse. I am helpless as I watch them.

The sirens roar and the ambulance eases down the shoulder, navigating the maze of stopped cars until we are no longer on the bridge and are racing toward the hospital.

As I stare at Jade, her body not responding to the compressions, I suddenly think of my father—and then my mother, staring at her Chromatic glasses with hurt and frustration.

NINETY-TWO

JADE'S BODY spasms and water spills from her lips as she starts to gasp for air. I reach for her hand, and she finds mine.

The EMTs stabilize her, and I am barely able to make out her face through my glassy eyes. I see only the glow of her skin and the damp red dress that clings to her body.

"Thank you," I say repeatedly to the EMTs, struggling to keep my composure.

I try not to think about how Donovan Scott had intended for us to die in that crash.

That's why he'd let us leave so easily.

NINETY-THREE

I sit next the hospital bed as Jade sleeps. A million thoughts run through my mind: could I prove he tried to kill us? What if he came for us again? What kind of life is it that you have to constantly look over your shoulder because people in power want you to suffer?

There is a part of me that feels that I deserve all of this. But Jade doesn't.

Some situations you can't undo, though. Jade and I made a pact only death can undo—that death almost *did* undo—but we are together, for better or worse.

NINETY-FOUR

JADE HAS BEEN awake and alert for more than an hour when she begins to ask the questions that yield the answers I have reached up to this point.

She seems incredulous that he would try to kill us, but the fact that we are in a hospital room shifts her perspective rather quickly.

"You'll never be able to prove he did it. And even if you did, I doubt anyone would have sympathy for us and what we did," she says.

I am reaching for possible solutions, but the only one that comes to mind is our running away.

NINETY-FIVE

JADE HAS no job to leave behind. I do.

She also has no family to leave behind. I do.

Still, to stay is to flaunt our relationship in front of a powerful man, who, all things considered, did nothing to deserve any of this.

Sure, he tried to eliminate us, and as much as I want to hate him for that, I understand his rationale.

Jade and I are now all we have. Whatever chapter comes next, it will be up to us.

When she is released from the hospital, we head to my apartment to plan our next steps.

NINETY-SIX

THERE IS NOT much in my apartment of any value, but it gives us a sanctuary to restore our strength.

Jade doesn't want to call the police about this anymore than I do.

"I just want to leave and start over somewhere where no one knows us or cares about any of this," she says.

I understand entirely. I am just trying to figure out where that is or if such a place exists.

"We need to go see my mother."

Between us, we have only Jade's phone and license and my phone and wallet.

We set out on foot.

NINETY-SEVEN

My MOTHER MEETS us at our usual restaurant, and I introduce her to Jade. She immediately embraces Jade, and Jade holds on to her. They've never met, but they cry as they hold each other, sharing a moment that will forever transcend my understanding.

"We have to leave, Mom." I explain everything and what Jade and I have decided.

"Well, you're going to need some money and a car," she responds. She then hands me her keys and the cash she has in her purse. "And when you get settled, I'll come to visit you."

I'm unable to stop crying.

NINETY-EIGHT

WE HUG MY MOTHER GOODBYE, as we stand on the stoop in front of her brownstone. I notice for the first time that she's wearing her glasses. Apparently she's finally reconciled her differences with them.

We pull away from the curb slowly, her reflection getting smaller and smaller in the rearview mirror as we reach the end of the street and turn onto the parkway.

For the moment this car is the only thing Jade and I own.

Our plan is to drive west, as far as we can go, then set up shop in a place we'll call home.

NINETY-NINE

MAYBE I WILL TEACH. Jade has mentioned her desire to paint. Before, she only worked with pencils and pens. Now she is looking to use her newfound discovery of colors to make a different kind of art. While there aren't many Chromats out there, many of them would pay a pretty penny for the kind of art Jade hopes to create.

We tell stories of our lives before becoming Chromats, passing the time, as we drive farther west, the sky opening up before us in splendid oranges, yellows, pinks, violets, and blues.

Surely there is something out there for us.

ONE HUNDRED

Two DAYS later we arrive in a small town at the foot of the mountains, just beyond the desert.

"Let's stop here," Jade says.

"Okay."

We don't even know the name of this town, but we know in our hearts that this will be our home, where we become the people we were always meant to be.

I call my mother to let her know we've arrived and that I'll give her more information later.

I don't know what kind of life we'll have here and whether we'll be successful, but we have each other—and that is worth everything.

ACKNOWLEDGMENTS

A special thank you to the following people: my wife and daughter, my parents, Torrey Holbrook Walker, Sabin Prentis, Grant Faulkner, Rion Amilcar Scott, Maurice Carlos Ruffin, Scott Semegran, Mitchell Davis, Amy Jones, Laurie Carter, Nia Forrester, Van G. Garrett, Tananarive Due, Nancy Stohlman, Chris L. Butler, and my creative writing students at Hampton University.

ALSO BY RAN WALKER

B-Sides and Remixes

30 Love: A Novel

Mojo's Guitar: A Novel / (Il était une fois Morris Jones)

Afro Nerd in Love: A Novella

The Keys of My Soul: A Novel

The Race of Races: A Novel

The Illest: A Novella

Bessie, Bop, or Bach: Collected Stories

Four Floors (with Sabin Prentis)

Black Hand Side: Stories

White Pages: A Novel

She Lives in My Lap

Reverb

Work-In-Progress

Daykeeper

Most of My Heroes Don't Appear On No Stamps

Portable Black Magic

The Strange Museum: 50-Word Stories

Bees + Things + Flowers: Microfictions

The World Is Yours: Microfictions

Can I Kick It?: Sneaker Microfiction and Poetry

The Golden Book: A 50-Year Marriage In 50-Word Stories

Keep It 100: 100-Word Stories

ABOUT THE AUTHOR

Ran Walker is the author of twenty-four books. He is the winner of the Indie Author Project's 2019 Indie Author of the Year Award, the 2019 Black Caucus of the ALA Fiction Ebook Award, the 2018 Virginia Author Project Award for Adult Fiction, and the 2021 Blind Corner Afrofuturism Microfiction Award. He teaches creative writing at Hampton University and at Writer's Digest University and lives with his wife and daughter in Virginia. He can be reached via his website, www.ranwalker.com.

* 9 7 8 1 0 2 0 0 0 1 2 5 3 *